Age-Gap Older-Man & Plus-Size Virgin

Dolliana Jeffries and Izzie Vee

Published by Dolliana Jeffries, 2024.

Table of Contents

Age-Gap Older-Man & Plus-Size Virgin Girl Erotca Short Story

Forbidden Biker MC Curvy Younger Woman Steamy Smutt
Book

Forced Erotic Romance, Dark Reverse Harem Naughty Virgin
DOLLIANA JEFFRIES[1] & IZZIE VEE[2]

---

1. https://www.amazon.com/s?k=dolliana+jeffries

2. https://www.amazon.com/
   s?k=izzie+vee&i=digital-text&crid=31LQJTEQYT2EE&sprefix=izzie+vee%2Cdigit
   al-text%2C121&ref=nb_sb_noss

Chapter 1

EVER SINCE I WAS ABLE to walk into a bar and buy my own drink, I'd had a crush on Colin Anderson.

The first time I saw him, he'd been sitting at the bar, drinking a beer. Once I caught sight of his face, I couldn't stop staring. I didn't know if it was his whiskey-colored eyes or his handsome face, but I'd suddenly discovered my liking for older men—him in particular.

He'd merely glanced my way, probably seeing me as too young in his eyes since he was probably twice my age. No matter how hard I tried to get his attention, he just wouldn't give me the time of day, and that broke my heart.

Fast forward four years later and I was finally done with college, ready to take on life by the balls. It was my first day back in my small town, Mercury, and all I wanted to do was head to that bar to see Colin again, if he was still even around.

I'd changed a lot–gaining a few pounds over the years that left me almost unrecognizable to some, seeing I was a twig for most of my life. Colin knew me as a twig; now, I didn't know if he'd even look my way. Maybe he wouldn't find me interesting at all—weight or not.

I sighed as I glanced at my thick thighs in the mirror. It was summer, and the only thing that felt right to be in were shorts and a loose top. I ran my hands down my hips, smiling at myself and content with the person I'd become physically and mentally.

College had taught me a lot, and the years had only made that better. Unlike some, there was no horror story about my college experience. I'd taken advantage of every opportunity and had as much fun as I possibly could.

I sighed heavily and went downstairs, where I saw my parents in the living room watching T.V. My little sister, Emma, was reading a book in a corner, seemingly out of touch with reality.

"Hey, I think I'm gonna take a walk up by the bar and chill for a bit," I said, capturing their attention.

Emma perked up suddenly in her chair. "Ouu, can I come."

"No, you may not," my mom inserted firmly. "You're not old enough."

She turned to run her gaze down my frame. "Don't you think that outfit is quite revealing?"

I smiled. "No, it's summer. I'll be back," I said.

"Okay, honey; just be careful," Dad said, glancing at me for a second before his eyes were back on the T.V.

"I will," I said before grabbing my keys and leaving the house. My parents were always the overprotective type—my mom especially, but had eased a little during college. I guess they finally realized I was not a kid who needed twenty-four-hour surveillance. Plus, the only bad thing that ever happened in this small town was bar fights—since there were a lot of those.

I pulled in a breath and smoothened my hands against my shorts before I hopped in my Camry and headed up the road. I could have walked if I wanted to, but it was late out, and the roads were usually too lonely for my taste.

I entered the small-town area shortly after, with the only place open at this time being the bar I was on my way to. As soon as it hit 9, the place was a ghost town, and I guess I'd forgotten what it was like after being away for college for so long.

A city like Los Angeles was a striking difference and had opened up my eyes to a load of things that I couldn't even have imagined being in Mercury. After enrolling in college there, I finally realized why my parents had tried to convince me to go elsewhere. They didn't want me exposed to certain things, but L.A. had held me by the arms and marched me forward. I'd developed a type of confidence I'd lacked being here.

Yet, Mercury was my home and would always be. I supposed there was nothing like getting up to fresh air in your lungs and peace and quiet. I'd been happy for the opportunity to explore a different place, but now that I've done that, it's time to head back to my small hometown, pining over a man I'd admired for years. I couldn't admit it to anyone, but Colin was my main reason for returning to Mercury.

I smiled as I approached the small bar, which was just a log cabin in the eyes of many, but for me, it was my favorite place in town. It was where I found Colin.

I stepped out, my boots hitting the graveled parking lot. Taking a deep breath, I closed my car door with a loud thud and scanned the surroundings. Not much had changed since I last left—the place was still filled with motorcycles since it was mostly a biker club than anything else. Being a small town, it seemed like everyone had taken advantage.

A smile tipped the corner of my lips when I glanced at the dingy old sign that read 'Mercury's Haven.' Around it were biker patches with their logo. I went further, hearing the 90s rock songs playing inside. It was almost like I never left, I thought, dragging my fingers along the aging wood engraved with a few names.

I paused when I saw the flapping 'hiring' sign attached to the door; the wind had blown off two ends of the paper, almost making it unnoticeable. I bit my lips and tapped my finger against it before I decided to go inside.

I pushed the door open, and the bell above me gave me away as I entered. All heads turned to me, and I was still smiling as I watched the eyes take me in. Most of the people I recognized, but I knew they didn't recognize me. No way would some of them look at me like this if they knew I was Wallace's kid. That man was respected a lot around these parts.

Though, I wasn't complaining. It was nice to get looks from men like this for once, instead of college boys. I bet their cocks were probably throbbing beneath their tight denim jeans. I was certainly the type of distraction these men hadn't seen in a while since the majority of the women around here were reserved housewives, and the rest were training to be.

Tonight wasn't a busy night, though; I'd expected it to be packed like it always was, no matter the day of the week.

The chatter increased as I walked to the front. Men smiled, tipped their beers at me, and I soaked it up like a dry sponge. I smiled back, rocking my hips from side to side, realizing there was no sign of Colin.

The disappointment I felt caused my smile to falter, seeing it was him I wanted to see, despite the attention from others. I narrowed my gaze ahead and walked to the counter, where I saw a man behind the counter with his back turned to me.

My brows furrowed as I wondered if it was Colin. He had the height, and the hair was still jet black, but why would Colin be behind the bar? He was always a customer.

My heart plummeted nonetheless because despite not seeing this man's face, the familiarity to Colin was enough to have my heart doing a few flips.

I planted my palm against the counter and slid on an empty stool around it. When my gaze lingered on his backside, I knew I couldn't be mistaken. I knew Colin's ass when I saw it—how could I not when I'd admired it for a year. He had the narrowest hips and the sexiest ass I'd ever seen on a man.

"Hello?" I said, my heart throbbing with anticipation as I waited for him to turn.

When he did, my breath hitched in my throat. It was him, alright. And the effect was still the same because here I was, the world a blur behind me while this man held the focus. It'd been three years, but he was still the same—looking like he'd just crawled out of a magazine with his handsome face, broad shoulders, and towering height. As my gaze trailed down his appealing frame, I wondered if he had a family by now. The last time I heard, he didn't. He was a Loner who'd preferred flings to commitment. At the time, that had been heartbreaking, but what did I expect at twenty-one?

He didn't have a dad-bod like most of the fathers in this town, though, so I guess that was something. If he had a family, I'd be devastated.

I couldn't take my eyes off him, and the more I stared, the more I realized he was staring back, his smoldering brown eyes pinned on me as he polished a glass. His gaze lingered on my chest before he tore his eyes away and focused on polishing his glass once again.

"What can I get you, ma'am?"

I couldn't help my smile if I wanted to. "Any beer will be fine," I said.

He nodded and went to fill the same glass he'd been busy polishing. I followed his every movement, noticing the lock of hair that dropped onto his forehead as he filled my glass.

He placed it in front of me, and I smiled, "Thank you." I held that glass, wishing he'd one day hold me like it instead.

"You're welcome," he said, flashing one last glance my way before he turned his back again and continued with his work.

I straightened in my chair and cleared my throat, thinking that the days of me just staring and remaining quiet were long over. If I wanted anything to happen with Colin, I had to stop being the girl I was at twenty-one.

"So I saw the hiring sign outside. You guys hiring?" I asked.

He paused what he was doing and turned to me yet again. I could never get tired of seeing his face.

"I am," he said, throwing the towel over his broad shoulders.

My brow raised. "You? You own here?" Last time I checked, it was an old man named Tim. "I thought it was an old guy with the tattoos."

A ghost of a smile crossed his lips before he said, "I bought it from him a year ago—just months before he became sick and went to live with his kids in Portland."

"Oh," I said as I took another sip of my beer. "Well, if you're hiring, I'd like to be considered for a position. I could write a resume or whatever if you prefer something more formal," I smiled.

He didn't take his eyes off me, which did nothing to improve my heart rate. "How old are you?"

"Twenty-five," I proudly said.

He rested his arms against the counter and leaned into me. I swallowed the lump in my throat as soon as a musky fragrance, blending wood, citrus, and a hint of vanilla, wafted towards me. Him being so close alerted every nerve inside my body, and in a split second, between my legs was tingling.

"Aren't you a bit too 'educated' to be looking for work in a bar?" He asked, his gaze searching my face.

"Well, the next best bet around here is a grocery store."

He scoffed, easing up, but his earlier question gave me reason to ponder.

"How do you even know I'm educated?"

"Aren't you the college kid? The whole town was buzzing when you went off to L.A for college."

I beamed at him. "They were?"

He nodded curtly. "Was the topic of conversation for a few months—apparently, you're one of the very few."

"Sounds sad when you say it like that."

He chuckled.

"I didn't–I didn't think you'd recognize me," I admitted, feeling the heat rise inside my body.

"No one can forget those bright green eyes, can they?" With that, he left to serve a man who approached the counter.

My heart lurched. So he did know who I was? That entire year I'd spent pining over him, thinking he didn't even see me or know who I was—when he had. He'd notice my eyes, and that was something.

"So why are you hiring anyway? You seem to be holding down this joint just fine," I said once he was free again.

He glanced at me. "People like a fresh face," he said. "I'll still be around, but during the busy nights."

I nodded. "Understood."

"Know anything about bartending, Katie?" He asked, catching me by surprise by knowing my name.

"You know my name?" I asked, feeling almost breathless.

"Like I said, you were once the talk of the town around here."

I folded my lips to catch my smile. I'd never been much around here except Wallace's shy kid. It was nice to know people knew who I was.

I looked at him. "Still, I wouldn't have thought you'd remember my name or even know who I was," I teased.

He said nothing. Someone else came and he attended to them while I drank my beer, unable to keep my eyes off him. He wore a leather jacket, but I knew those bulky arms were filled with tattoos. I wanted to see them again; I wanted to admire his mouth-watering physique even more.

Colin was probably forty by now, but he didn't look a day over thirty years old. Guys his age in this town usually had a beer belly or had gotten too out of shape to be deemed attractive. Then there were the younger ones, who were usually on the skinnier side. That's why Colin stood out so much to me or anyone else. He was different.

When he came to Mercury, the town had been in a frenzy. Every woman wanted him—married or not, and every girl, like myself, wanted him to look their way.

Of course, Colin had taken advantage of the attention he'd gotten and had left this bar every night with a new woman at his arm—or at least so I heard. That broke my heart, but I never gave up on Colin being mine one day. Still didn't.

I ordered another beer while Colin chatted up a few of his friends at the counter. I wanted his attention to be on me—I wanted him to chat with me for the entire night until I was too drunk to head home. Maybe he'd take me home; I'd make a move on him—kiss him for the first time.

Who knew? Tonight was filled with possibilities.

But I didn't get further than two beers before my phone started ringing, and at a glance, I realized it was my mom.

I felt the heat on my cheeks as I glanced at Colin, who looked my way. I timidly placed the phone to my ear and answered.

"Where are you?" She immediately asked.

"I told you where I'd be," I said.

"It's approaching midnight. What are you doing out so late?" She asked, an edge to her voice.

"Mom, this is Mercury, not L.A. I'll be fine, and I'm not a kid."

"As long as you're staying in my house, you are, young lady," she snapped.

I rolled my eyes, teeth clenching before I hung up. Feeling annoyed that my mom had pissed on my beautiful night, I slid from around the counter and decided to head out. Just like that, everything I'd felt was replaced by anger.

I stormed through the door and sighed once I got out. I raked my fingers through my hair and took in a whiff of the fresh air. If things were going to continue like this, then I'd have to go in search of an apartment as well as a job.

I was about to pull my car door open when the door to the bar opened, and Colin stepped outside. My heart rejoiced in my chest seeing him, and I froze, my hands tightening around my keys.

"You're leaving?" He asked.

"Yeah, it's getting late."

He walked towards me, his eyes roaming my frame.

"I thought you'd want to hear more about the vacancy."

My brows raised. "You're interested in hiring me?" I asked, shocked.

"Only if you're serious about the position," he said, stopping in front of me. The wind blowing against him only made his cologne more potent.

I nodded. "Of course I am," I was quick to say.

"What do you know about being a bartender anyway?" He asked, leaning against my car.

"Enough to know that they'll keep coming back."

"Can you even make a cocktail, Katie?"

I swallowed, looking up at him. "They barely drink that stuff around here. It's always beer, whiskey, gin, and scotch."

He smiled—a straight line of perfectly white teeth. "Good answer. Either way, I'll do whatever mixing needs to be done until you learn how to."

"You're saying I'm hired?"

"I'm saying I'm willing to give you a trial run," he said.

I was smiling hard. "That sounds good," I chirped.

"Come by around five tomorrow. I open at six, but I want to show you around the place and give you a few tips before you start."

My mouth hung open. "I– I start tomorrow?"

"You start tomorrow," he clarified.

I laughed. "WOW, okay. Thank you. I'll be there."

Our gazes met, and my nipples instantly tightened beneath my shirt. Colin's gaze dropped to my lips, and I pulled in a sharp breath, breaking the silence between us.

"See you then," he said before he turned and left.

"Fuck!" I hissed once he disappeared into the bar.

Chapter 2

I WAS ALL READY TO go by 4:30 the next day, fully dressed and prepared. I hardly got any sleep last night, couldn't stop thinking about Colin and our conversation, his cologne, and how handsome he is.

I'd replayed every bit of detail in my head, almost finding it hard to believe that I'd even had a conversation with the man. Now, I'd be working for him to make things even better.

I ran downstairs, my body packed with adrenaline. My parents were in the living room watching their favorite evening show. Their heads turned in unison when they saw me standing there.

Mom's gaze did a once over of me, her brows furrowing. "Shorts again? Where are you off to?" She asked.

"My new job," I said.

It was Dad's time to frown. "You got a job? Where?"

"Er... at Mercury's Haven," I smiled, knowing what was to come.

Dad scoffed. "The biker bar in town?"

I nodded.

"Absolutely not!" Mom shrieked.

I blew out a breath. "It's happening, Mom, and I start in less than thirty minutes, so if you don't mind." I was about to head out when my mom's voice stopped me.

"What was the point of college if you're gonna waste away at the local bar?"

I frowned. "What was the point of college if I had to return to this town at the end of it?" I snapped back.

She looked baffled, her lips moving for a few seconds without words. "You could easily get a job at that insurance place up the road," she argued.

"Right. With the five people who've been there since I was born," I quipped.

"You're not working at that bar, young lady," Dad hissed.

"I'm not asking for permission, Dad," I said.

They both looked taken aback.

"If you leave this house, don't think about coming back. That place is filled with fucking low-lives."

"That's not true!"

"Your choice if you want to become one," he said before he spun his head back towards the television and continued watching, a pout on his face.

I looked between them and knew that I'd be going back and forth with them for the rest of my life if I didn't put my foot down.

"Then I'd be here to get my things tonight," I said before I turned on my heels and headed towards the door. Their gasps were the last thing I heard, followed by the rattling slam of the door.

My throat tightened with emotions, but I straightened up and went straight to my car. There was a possibility that I'd find my luggage at the door tonight, but I didn't mind. I wasn't going to allow them to get in the way of me and Colin.

The laughable part was that there was no 'me and Colin', but I already saw where it could be a possibility. I just hoped the cash I had saved would get me someplace to rent somewhere around here if it came to that.

I PULLED IN A SHAKY breath when I parked outside Colin's bar. The front door was closed, but his Harley Davidson motorcycle was parked outside, indicating that he was inside.

Tucking my hair behind my ear, I pushed my car door open and stepped out. I quickly glanced down at my attire, though it was similar to what I'd worn the previous day—only I was showing a lot more cleavage today, which I thought was good for working in a bar. And for Colin.

I smiled as I approached the bar and pushed the door. I was happy when it opened and got even happier when I stepped inside and saw Colin around the counter.

"You're right on time."

"Well, I couldn't be late on my first day," I smiled as I moved towards him.

"For a second, I thought you wouldn't show," he said, his voice low.

"Trust me, I've been thinking about this all night. There's nothing I wanted more." Except him.

He had that pleasant look on his face, though there wasn't a distinct smile in place.

"So, the job's not hard. You provide their drinks, they pay, and everyone's happy. There's a price list under the counter for reference."

I circled the counter to join him, my pulse increasing with each step I took.

"The most important thing to remember is that people come to bars for the experience, too, not just the drinks. You must always be pleasant and engaging—even if you don't feel like it."

I smiled. "How do you think I am in that department?" He paused to look at me, his gaze searching.

"I don't know. I guess I'll have to see," he said.

I raised a brow. "Fair enough."

"It helps that you're already pretty. You don't have to do too much," he said as he reached to grab two bottles of beer.

I beamed at his broad back, my cheeks hot from a blush. "You think I'm pretty."

He handed me a bottle. "I'm not blind, Katie. Neither are you."

I giggled a bit. "I guess it just feels good to hear it from someone as attractive as you."

He met my gaze. "Hmm." He took a gulp of his beer before resting it on the counter. "Next thing, you have to be able to multitask. People will come at you from all angles when it's busy. It may be overwhelming for you."

"I think I can manage."

"I really need to know that you will."

He walked off and headed towards the back of the bar. I quickly followed behind him, almost bumping into him when he stopped abruptly at the door.

As soon as he entered, I realized it was a bedroom, and my heart plummeted for some reason.

"Tim used to crash here a lot. If someone's too wasted to get home, I usually let them sleep it off here, so if something like that ever happens, you're more than welcome to offer," he said, turning to me.

I swallowed the lump in my throat. Being so close to him did things to my body, and the fact that we were in an empty room didn't make matters better. My flesh tingled, that warm sensation flooding my body each time he looked at me.

"Er, yeah," I said, scratching my forehead.

"Well, that should be it. You can start by cleaning the tables before I open up," he said.

I quickly nodded, taking a step back and out of the room. It finally felt like the oxygen had returned to my lungs once I stepped out. I hastily moved behind the counter and took the rag I'd seen there earlier before I headed out to the sitting area.

Colin was busy behind the counter doing whatever while I wiped at tables that were almost spotless.

It was just him and me in this bar, and a part of me wanted to make a move, which had been the idea from the very start. But I found that my ideas couldn't be put in motion as easily as they'd come in my head.

Colin was different, and I didn't want to scare him away by being too easy. However, from my past observations, he usually liked easy. The thing was, I wasn't sure he'd like me. What if he didn't find me attractive? Yes, he'd looked at me like he wanted to fuck me in front of a crowd of people, but I could be wrong about that too.

What if I was just allowing myself to see and feel things that weren't even there? What if all Colin saw in me was the girl everyone had spoken about after I'd gone off to college?

I sighed and paused, wiping, hating that I was at this point again where I questioned everything about Colin and the possibility of us being together. Him fucking me, if I was being frank.

I didn't want to be that twenty-one-year-old virgin girl, drooling after a man and not putting in any effort to attract him. I wanted to be the person I'd become during college. That was who I wanted to show.

I turned to him and was surprised when I caught him staring at me. "Hey, have you ever dated someone younger than you?"

His thick brows furrowed. "Why?"

I shrugged. "Just curious."

"I don't date below twenty," he said.

So that meant he'd have dated me when I first saw him here, then? My back straightened as I became more hopeful.

"What's the youngest you've ever dated?" I asked.

"What's with the questions?"

I shrugged. "I'd just like to know more about my boss."

"My dating life?" He raised a brow, brown eyes curious.

"It's a part of you, isn't it?" I jabbed.

"It's private," he said, and by the tone of his voice, I knew he was serious.

"Sorry."

"It's fine," he said, and I swallowed the lump in my throat, trying to rid myself of the bit of embarrassment that coursed through me. I decided not to say anything more and continued wiping the tables until I was done.

I returned behind the counter to put the rag away and was about to wash my hands when Colin's question had me pausing.

"What's your motive here, Katie?"

I looked at him. "What do you mean?"

"I'm sensing this isn't just about wanting a job here," he said, trapping me with his gaze.

"What makes you think that?"

He didn't answer, but the look in his eyes told me he knew exactly what was happening here. I bit my lips and dropped my gaze, searching the floor as I thought about what to say next.

"What if you're right?" I asked, my heart galloping as I returned my gaze to him.

His Adam's apple bobbed. "Then you're playing a very dangerous game," he said.

A knock suddenly came at the door, and I gasped, my head swiveling towards the door. An elderly man came pushing through, a stained smile in place as he waved at us.

"I figured you wouldn't be open as yet, but I saw two vehicles parked outside and thought I'd try my luck," he chuckled as he approached.

"We're just about to open," Colin said as he sidestepped me and went to attend to the man.

I blew out a breath, rushing to the bathroom to get some water on my face. I was way too hot.

Chapter 3

IT WAS A FRIDAY, AND the bar was fuller than I'd like for my first day. I didn't even have time to take a good glimpse of Colin, and after our conversation earlier, I wanted to read the look on his face. But he was busy, and so was I.

People took full advantage of the weekend; men laughed, chattered, and sang along to their favorite music that blasted from the speakers.

I noticed the way many of them looked at me. By now, I knew most would have figured out who I was, and the looks on their faces told me exactly that. Surely, they couldn't believe Wallace's scholar was home and working in a bar. Since, according to them, only prostitutes worked at places like this. The close-mindedness in this place was simply appalling, and I was happy that I'd gotten the chance to explore something more.

Whether or not people found that as a waste of my parents' money, was simply their business, people in Mercury had nothing better to do but gossip, and right now, I was the hot topic, but next week, it'd probably be someone else and their cheating husband.

The rush died down at around nine. People came and went, but I wasn't as busy going back and forth as I'd been earlier.

A middle-aged woman approached the bar, and by the way she looked at me, I knew I was her target. I recognized her as I did everyone else in this town. She was the leader of a book club my mom used to attend during my high school years.

She smiled at me, but I knew it was as fake as a tan in January. I smiled back until she was in front of me, leaning over the counter.

"You're Cherry's girl, aren't you?"

"That's right, ma'am," I replied, holding my smile.

Her gaze went from my open cleavage to my face and back. "You've... grown."

"It'd be unnatural if I hadn't."

"Hmm, I didn't know you got back from college." I'm sure she did.

"Just the other day," I offered.

"Half of us thought you'd stick to the city life. You know, they say you never come back once you go there."

"I'm living testimony that's not true. I like Mercury."

"Hmm, I see you've gotten some of the influence from there, though." Her gaze faltered to my cleavage again, a slightly disgusted look on her face.

"Of course," I chimed. "In fact, I feel like a new woman. You wouldn't believe the things they do in the City."

Her cheeks reddened. "Oh, I can just imagine."

"Er, how's your daughter Gretchen? I heard she's on her fourth kid, still not married and under thirty." I made a sad face.

She gasped, her face instantly gone pale. She worked her mouth to say something but clamped it shut and spun on her heels before she marched back to her group at the far end. They immediately began gossiping, looking my way, and I knew it was about me.

I smiled, satisfied with myself for not allowing her to intimidate me. It was safe to say, I came a long way.

"What did I say about engagement?" Colin asked. I almost jumped at the sound of his voice, but once I saw the look on his face, I knew I had nothing to worry about. He seemed amused.

"I was being pleasant," I pointed out.

A small smile tipped the corner of his lips before he left to attend to his customers.

THE BAR CAME DOWN TO one drunk who sat in a corner. His hand trembled as he brought the beer to his lips, one arm pinned to the rim of the table as he tried to balance himself.

I watched with a frown, my brows perking up when he looked towards the counter, hand raised.

"Another, please," he said, words slurred.

I scoffed as I looked at Colin, who seemed to be observing him with the same intensity.

"That's all for tonight, James. Best you head on your way."

He grunted, slamming the empty bottle to the table and causing it to crash against the others that were piled onto there.

"Y–you people are no fucking fun," he said as he got up, leaning against the chair and causing it to tip over. He almost went with it, but luckily, the table was there to keep him up.

He swaggered to the front door, holding onto everything he passed to keep his balance.

I grinned as I looked at Colin. "Aren't you gonna offer the back room?" I asked.

"He lives two steps away from here. He'll be fine," he said as he immediately began cleaning up. I sighed heavily, looking at the messy tables and the messy floors. It was some minutes past eleven, and that was a new record for me in Mercury. Plus, as much as I hated to admit it, I was exhausted.

"You can head home; I'll clean up here," he said as if reading my thoughts.

"I wouldn't be much of an employee if I allowed you to do that," I smiled, grabbing a rag from beneath the counter and rushing to the sitting area.

I immediately began collecting bottles and wiping in between.

"You did good today. Surprisingly better than I'd expected."

I paused what I was doing to look at him, a smile on my face. "You think so?"

He nodded, "I do."

"I'm glad."

I continued to wipe and clean up, and surprisingly, I was done in no time. All I wanted now was a shower and a bed.

"I should get going. I'll see you tomorrow," I told Colin while grabbing my things.

Deep down, I wanted to make a move on him, but I knew that if things were to escalate, I wouldn't have the strength to go the extra mile.

"I'll see you tomorrow," he said; I smiled and then went on my way.

I sighed a resigned sigh as soon as I stepped outside and felt the cool wind against my face. I'd passed up opportunities to make a move but figured I'd let this one slide until the next day.

I wasn't used to being on my feet for so long, and all I wanted to do was sleep.

I hopped in my van and started the ignition. I gasped when the engine didn't come to life, no matter how many times I twisted the key.

I sighed heavily and flopped back against the seats, feeling slightly annoyed. But as soon as I looked towards the shop, I realized Colin might be the perfect person to help me.

I quickly got up and went back inside the bar. He was coming from around the counter when I entered.

"Er, my car won't start," I informed.

His thick brow raised as he approached me. "Could you take a look?"

"Sure," he said as he moved past me. He stepped inside my car, looking quite uncomfortable as he fitted his huge frame inside. He tried to start it again, but when that didn't work, he went outside, pulled the hood up, and took a look at the engine.

He rubbed the nape of his neck before he looked at me. "I don't know, Katie. My specialty's not really cars, but it could be a spark plug issue."

I sighed heavily. "Just my luck," I murmured.

"It's late now, but I could call a mechanic out tomorrow to have him take a look."

"I'd really appreciate that, but the problem is getting home now."

"There's no problem; I could take you home."

I glanced at his motorcycle. "On that?"

"You have a better idea?"

I swallowed. "No, I've just never ridden on a motorcycle before," I confessed.

He shrugged his shoulders a little. "First time for everything," he said as he closed the hood and moved towards his motorcycle.

I closed my doors before I quickly moved in his direction. Colin handed me his helmet, and with a hammering heart, I allowed him to strap me in. My body was just mere inches away from his, which was probably the closest we'd ever been.

"What'll you wear?" I asked.

"I'll take my chances," he said as he climbed onto the motorcycle and brought it to life.

I stared at him and the beast beneath him, wondering if I even had it in me to join. As much as I'd been spontaneous in L.A., I'd never ridden on a motorcycle before. That was new to me.

He glanced at me. "Coming?"

I quickly nodded before I moved towards him, held onto his shoulder, and climbed onto the motorcycle.

"Hold on," he said.

Knots formed inside my stomach as I wrapped my hands around his firm stomach, feeling the warmth of his skin against me.

I swallowed hard, feeling the tingling between my legs that were brushing against his. When the motorcycle began moving, my hands tightened around Colin, a cocktail of nerves stirring in my body as the motorcycle sped down the empty stretch of road. I clung to Colin tightly, purely out of fear of falling off and nothing else, but in doing so, I felt things. Things that seemed to multiply now that I was able to touch him. It was like everything had suddenly become better. I leaned into him, my tits brushing against his back, my bare legs rubbing against his denim jeans.

I smiled, feeling the tension ease from my limbs the longer he rode. Shortly after, I felt like letting go and embracing the ride, but I also wanted to cling to Colin for as long as I could.

As we approached my house, the bike slowed before it came to a stop. It took me a second to collect myself, but when I finally climbed off, I staggered a little, smiling at him to distract him from my embarrassment.

"Thank you," I said, releasing the strap from under my chin before handing him his helmet.

"Don't mention it. I'll see you tomorrow."

"Sure thing," I said.

He nodded before he strapped on his helmet and rode off into the pitch-black night. I sighed dreamily, watching him until he could no longer be seen. After that, I pulled my keys out and headed inside, happy that my luggage wasn't at the door as I'd suspected.

Chapter 4

I WOKE UP FROM MY SLEEP the following morning when my mom barged in, hands akimbo as she stared down at me with a frown on her face.

I frowned, too, wondering what the problem was now while I eased up in the bed, rubbing my eyes.

"What is it?" I asked, feigning a sigh.

"What's gotten into you?" She snapped, her expression filled with disgust.

"Wh–"

"You can't guess who called me just now talking about how rude you were at that bar."

I sighed, knowing who exactly she'd gotten the call from.

"I wasn't being rude to anyone?" I defended, throwing the sheets from around me as I climbed out of bed.

"I'm sure Cecile wouldn't lie–"

"And I would?" I asked, suddenly curious.

She crossed her arms now, rather defiantly. "I can't say I like the person you're becoming."

I raised a brow at that. "Just because I'm not in the habit of taking shit from people like I used to?" I contended.

"Watch your mouth, young lady," she exclaimed, her tone deepening.

"At some point, you have to realize I'm no longer a kid, and my purpose isn't to impress anyone in Mercury."

"These people talked so highly of you when you moved for college. It's quite the slap to the face knowing you have an attitude towards them."

I scoffed. "Let's admit that the only reason they even spoke about me is because they have nothing else to talk about," I murmured.

She gasped. "What's gotten into you? This is surely not the little girl I raised."

A brow perked up at that, but I refused to answer.

"I told your father it was a mistake sending you off to that college in the city."

"For Christ's sake, that school was the best thing that happened to me. If it weren't for it, I'd still be here, too shy to even lift my head from the ground and too boxed in to consider the endless possibilities that exist."

"Oh, and I reckon those possibilities include you working in a bar for a man who came to this place just three or four years ago?"

"And what's wrong with that?" I asked, grabbing my towel from a chair and turning to face her.

"You talk so highly of college, yet is that where you want to spend the rest of your life? Quite contradicting if you ask me."

"Who said anything about spending the rest of my life there? All I want is to save enough money so I could get my own place, and then who knows..."

She seemed taken aback at that. "Whatever path you're heading down, you better stop and make sure this is what you really want because you may feel like you have everything under control now, but I promise you, none of this is ever like sunshine and rainbows."

I pulled in a breath. "Thanks, Mom, but I think I'll take my chances," I said.

She nodded as if processing everything. Afterward, she cast me one last glance and went through the door, sealing it with a firm shut.

I sighed once again, knowing that it would only get worse from here. Each day of working for Colin would only lead to constant arguments, which made me more certain that I couldn't be here for long.

I SPOTTED COLIN AS soon as I entered the bar. I sucked in a breath and made my way towards the counter where he was. His head lifted to stare at me, his gaze lingering. I was suddenly happy that I'd chosen this top today. The material was soft and almost silky, the cleavage deep, showing a bit of my chest that wasn't confined by a bra.

My nipples tightened as I moved towards him, and his Adam's apple visibly bobbed before he looked away.

"Right on time," he said and now it was my time to fully take in his appearance. He wore a sleeveless vest, patches of his biker club stitched to it. His arms were out, and for the first time in a while, I got to see his tattoos, which held no color. Just pure black markings that ran down his strong arms, stopping at his wrist. As he wiped his hands into a towel, his muscles flexed, and I could feel the tiny beads of sweat forming on my forehead, and a rush of intense heat consumed my body.

His stubble was lower today, too, somewhat making him appear much younger than he was. His hair was the same mass of wavy dark hair, fuller at the top and slightly faded at the sides.

I cleared my throat. "Going somewhere?" I asked when he rounded the counter and stopped in front of me. It did nothing to help my galloping pulse.

"Me and some of the boys are taking a ride out of town for a bit. We should be back before closing, though, so don't worry about that part."

I swallowed. "Sounds fun."

He nodded, about to step away. On impulse, I grabbed his hand, taking myself by surprise. Colin glanced at my hand on his wrist before he looked at me. My lips moved, but the words were seemingly too afraid to leave my lips.

I clamped it back shut and decided to try again. "I just wanted to say thanks again for the job."

"There was no one better," he said with my hand still wrapped around his, too small to meet. This was the first time I'd ever held his hand, and I didn't want to let go. I felt the strength in his strong hand and wanted them around me—plain and simple. Plus, to my surprise, Colin looked at me like he didn't want me to let go either.

I took a step towards him, my heart in my throat, deciding that it was now or later. The way my heart was beating and the heat circling around me, I knew I had to bet on now.

Every inch of my body wanted this.

I went on my tiptoes, my lips parting as they neared his. I gasped when he held me at the nape of my neck and pulled me into him. Before I could even process my thoughts, his lips were crashed to mine, and I was moaning beneath him, trying to get my mouth to cooperate. I needed a second to get over the shock of Colin's hasty possession. His tongue was in my mouth, stroking me, and for a second, I wondered if it was a dream.

My heart rejoiced in my chest when he still continued to kiss me, and the flesh between my legs throbbed at a sweet beat as Colin took charge. I wrapped my hand around his neck, the other around his waist as my tongue danced with his, lapping and sucking, stroking every inch of my mouth while I explored his. He tasted like fresh spring water, and at the moment, I was quite thirsty for more of his touch.

His stubble grazed my skin, adding to the roughness of the kiss, his body heat radiating on me—his scent rubbing off from his body being pressed to mine.

I moaned, my eyes completely closed as I basked in the experience of Colin's kiss. I'd dreamt of this moment for a long time before now, but never did I imagine it would be like this. I was hungry for Colin, and the more I kissed him, the more I wanted his tongue for myself, the more my pussy throbbed for his tongue.

He pulled on my lips before he caressed them with his skillful tongue. Desperate to have him, I pressed my body closer to his, but I was already so close that there wasn't much further I could go.

Colin caught me by surprise when he lifted me from the floor, his hands resting under my ass as he carried me to the pool table. I latched my mouth to his again and kissed him before he placed me to the surface.

I didn't know what was about to happen, but I knew I was ready for it. I peeled the thin straps of my blouse from my shoulders and allowed them to fall around me. Colin broke the kiss to look down at me, his eyes dark as he stared at my naked breasts.

I watched the expression on his face—how he consumed my body with his hungry stare. That alone made me pool more juices for him; my panties were definitely sodden with juices.

"You're killing me here, Katie," he said, his voice raspy with emotions.

"I want to do the complete opposite," I said, reaching for him. He covered both my breasts with his huge hands, and I closed my eyes at the warmth that moved through my body at his touch.

I arched my back, and Colin lowered himself, pushing me further back on the table before he covered my nipple with his hot mouth. I gasped, throwing my head back as he alternated between sucking my full breasts. He stimulated my nipples with the tip of his tongue, circling and probing before he sucked on them.

I gasped, spreading my legs even further as he rested between them. I wished nothing separated us so Colin could just slip his cock inside me and fill me all the way.

I reached for his buckle, wanting him to do just that, but just then, a phone rang, and since mine was on silent, I knew it had to be his.

"Don't answer that," I said, my finger raking through his hair, holding him in place.

He moaned before he tore himself off me and reached into his pocket.

"I have to," he said as he answered. He didn't move, though, while he talked. I stared at him like a hungry predator, my eyes widening when I saw the huge bulge straining against his clad denim pants.

I bit my lips and reached for his buckle while he spoke to who I assumed were his biker friends, judging by the conversation.

Colin didn't protest as I released his buckle and pulled down his zipper. His hard-on was already trying to breach past his zipper as soon as I pulled it down. My mouth salivated as I hooked my fingers into the waistband and pulled down his pants.

I looked up at Colin and realized his gaze was steadily planted on me, but there was still no protest on his side, which, for me, meant I should continue.

He had black boxers on, which was quite a sexy sight around his toned legs. I ran my palm over his bulge and heard the little grunt that he quickly suffocated as he continued with the conversation.

Not wanting him to have second thoughts about any of this, I pulled down his boxers, gasping when his length sprang free. He was big and beautiful, lined with thick veins that led up to the round head.

Colin took a step back, and I slid from the pool table and to my knees, in line with his throbbing cock. I could spend all of eternity admiring it, but right now, I wanted to taste it more than anything else. Plus, the clock was already ticking.

I licked across my palm, then used that hand to massage his cock back and forth. I was shocked when he hardened even more in my hand like a steel pipe.

I moaned and began licking him from the base of his cock to the tip. I didn't stop until his length glistened with my saliva, his cock fully hard.

"You have about five minutes," he said to me before he threw his phone to the pool table. My heart lurched in my chest knowing I had five minutes to make him come inside my mouth.

I slipped his hard tip in my mouth, his length moving further down until I felt his tip at the back of my throat. Yet that wasn't all of him.

I pulled off, staring up at him and noting the fire in his eyes as he looked down at me. My heart raced, filling with an undeniable need to please him. I held him and used my tongue to tease the tiny hole at the tip.

He groaned, his hand reaching down to stroke through my hair. "You're so sexy... such a little minx."

My heart lurched at the name.

"Do you like when I call you that?" He asked, and I looked up at him, smiling.

"I'd love if you called me that more often," I grinned before I took him in my mouth again.

I started to move back and forth on his cock, my lips sliding against his rigid length while my mouth filled with saliva.

"Oh yes, that's it, baby," he said, his hand at the back of my head.

I paused and allowed him to take the lead, which he did. Colin thrust inside my mouth, powerfully fucking my mouth, his cock going further down my throat each time.

My cheeks stung with heat, and saliva dribbled down the corner of my mouth, but it was so good hearing his grunts, feeling as he used my mouth to pleasure himself.

I held onto his legs as his thrusts became faster. The sloppy sounds of him in my mouth filled the silence in the room, and as tears welled up in my eyes, I wanted to smile. This was more than what I dreamt of. Dreams couldn't come close to this reality.

He slowed, and then he withdrew his cock, pulling it in his hand before he slapped it against my mouth. I gasped, my eyes fluttering as his thick cock slapped my face.

With a grunt, he slipped it back inside my mouth, thrusting it so far I felt him down my throat. My nose was pressed to his pelvis, and he made me stay there while my throat constricted around him.

"Fuck, that's good," he groaned before he muttered a curse and pulled out.

"Where do you want it?" He asked me, his teeth clenched.

"Anywhere you do," I said.

While I tried to catch my breath, he quickly pulled his cock into his hands, and before long, a spray of his cum fell across my face. Colin muttered a curse, and I opened my mouth wide while threads of thick cum spilled across my mouth.

"Fucking perfect," he said, and I attempted to smile, my mouth still wide open.

My head swiveled towards the bar door when the bell above it sounded. I gasped, quickly scrambling to get myself together when a man around Colin's age stepped through.

"Oh fucking hell—I didn't–"

"Get out!" Colin exclaimed while pulling up his pants. The man almost stumbled as he quickly turned and left.

I was on the floor behind the pool table, just a single strap drawn over my shoulders while cum still ran down my face. My heart continued to pound in my chest; my gaze fixated on the door as I replayed the scene in my head.

"Fuck!" Colin grumbled as he moved towards the door and closed it.

I didn't realize I was shaking until he knelt before me and touched me on the arm. I gasped, my gaze flashing towards him.

"Are you okay?" He asked, the look in his eyes soft.

I shook my head, wiping my face with the back of my hand. "I—I—the entire Mercury will know what just happened between us. News spreads like fucking wildfire in this town," I gasped. "My parents will surely disown me."

"I'll take care of it. I know him; I'll talk to him, and everything will be fine."

I pulled in a breath, my hands still shaking.

Colin's grip tightened reassuringly on me. "Do you trust me?"

I met his gaze, and just like that, I felt like submitting to him. "Yes," I said, and there was no second-guessing it either. I realized I did. I'd yet to find out whether it would be to my detriment for me or not.

"Good. I've got it covered," he said, standing and stretching his hand out for me to take it.

I did and got up from the floor. Colin helped me to fix the strap of my blouse before he flashed me a wicked grin.

"You surprise me, Katie."

My cheeks warmed. "I could say the same."

He smiled, tracing his thumb across my lips. "I've gotta go, but I'll see you later."

I nodded, watching him pick up his phone and walk through the door. My heart was still hammering, but he'd given me enough reassurance to make me feel like everything would be okay—despite being caught with him glazing his cum across my face.

I should still feel some kind of devastation, but the happiness that bubbled in my gut outweighed every other feeling. It was only up from here.

Chapter 5

ALL THROUGHOUT THE night, my gaze kept moving towards the door inside the crowded bar. It reminded me of being caught with Colin earlier, but more than anything, I constantly looked because, this time, I wanted Colin to walk through those doors, and my stomach was in knots, stirring with anticipation as I looked forward to seeing his face again.

I'd expected tonight to be hectic without him, but it wasn't. People still whispered, which I knew would last for as long as I lived here, and I surely didn't give a damn at this point in my life. But today, it bugged me a little because, in the back of my mind, I couldn't help but wonder if the whispers were about me working here or the fact that Colin hadn't managed to stop that man from telling the whole town about us earlier.

The thoughts were fleeting, though, after I quickly realized the looks weren't from disgust. If they found out about what had happened earlier, they'd surely be clutching their invisible pearls or forming a committee to banish me from the town.

I smiled to myself despite my current situation. The only reason I cared about that man blabbering was because of my parents. Their opinion on my life had mattered less since I'd been back, but I still respected them a great deal and knew that if this got out, they'd be more embarrassed than me. I didn't want that for them.

"Katie Gardener?" I heard my name and turned to the side to find a group of three boys—well, men, since they were older than me but had slender athletic builds.

"Hi?" I said, looking between them. Realization dawned the longer I looked at their faces and realized they were old high school classmates.

"Hi!"

"Wow, you've...changed," the middle one said as his eyes trailed down my frame.

I smiled. "That's a good thing, right?" I asked.

He beamed. "Certainly is. I remember you were this puny little thing, head buried in the ground all the time," he chuckled, and the others joined in.

"Heard you left for the big city, though. That must've been fun," the other said as he observed me with the same thoroughness.

"It was."

"You look good, Katie; I'm not even gonna lie," the other one said.

"Thank you, Jake," I said as soon as his name came to me. His eyes lit up once he realized I recognized him.

"Could we buy you a drink?"

"Can't drink on the job, boys; I'm sorry."

They looked disappointed. "Well, that's sucks."

I smiled.

"So, what's the City like?" Jake asked as he pulled up a chair. "Could you get us three beers?"

I nodded as I got them three bottles from the refrigerator. I rested my elbows against the counter, giving them my full attention. It wasn't my intention, but I realized I'd only managed to push my breasts up in the process, causing their hungry eyes to follow.

I eased up and cleared my throat. "Well, it's big. Mercury would get lost in a place like LA, for sure. The city's always alive twenty-four-seven, and there's always something to do. Plus, the people mind their own businesses there."

They all laughed. "Sounds like heaven to me."

"Comes close."

"So why did you come back to Mercury? This place is as inviting as a porcupine in a balloon factory," Jake said, scoffing.

"You're right," I confessed.

"If I ever got the chance to get away from here, I'd walk the distance."

I grinned. "So why don't you, Jake?"

"Well, a guy like me wouldn't know what to do in the city. I'd probably make a fool of myself. Plus, my dad wants me to work on the farm—take over things when he's retired," he shrugged, taking a swig of his beer.

"Well, that's not living if that's not the life you want, is it?" I raised a brow.

He nodded. "And what about you? You're back here because of what your parents want too, isn't it?"

Just then, the bell dinged, and my eyes moved towards the door where Colin entered. My heart fluttered.

I smiled. "Mostly because of what I want, too."

"Well, if you plan on staying around here, I wouldn't mind seeing more of your pretty face," he smiled.

I grinned, deciding to indulge him. "If you make a habit of coming to this bar, you just might."

His smile broadened. "Noted, ma'am."

"Katie!"

I jumped when Colin's loud growl sounded behind me. I turned my body towards his, my pulse racing when I saw the lethal expression on his face. He looked like he could kill.

"Back... now," he said before he stepped off, already moving around the back.

I swallowed the lump in my throat, following behind him without even thinking to excuse myself from Jake and his friends. Colin led the way to the small office around the back. When I entered, he was inside, waiting for me, his mouth drawn into a grim line, his thick brows furrowed, his eyes dark.

"What are you doing?" He roared.

"Wha–I was just chatting to customers," I said, confused.

"You mean flirting?"

"I wasn't–"

"I heard what you said to that boy," he said, voice slightly lowered to bring across the fury in his tone.

I swallowed. "I was just being friendly."

He took a step towards me, and I almost gasped from being so close to him—his scent bringing me back to him, having his hard cock inside my mouth.

"I don't like it, and if you don't want me to break one of their scrawny necks, you'll stop it." With that, he sidestepped me and went through the door.

I gasped at his departure and the words he'd left me with. I didn't know what to make of them, but the way they made me feel was something else entirely. It made me hot and bothered, and I wondered if that was Colin being professional or jealous.

I bit my lips as I thought about the latter. It couldn't be, but I could feel the steam blazing off him and knew that there wasn't any professional rule I was breaking. He was jealous, and I couldn't help but giggle.

Possessive Colin was something I'd not been expecting, but it made me more aroused than I could have been if I'd touched myself. I glanced at the tiny wall clock at one corner of the room.

Half an hour to go.

With that, I smiled and left the door. Colin was serving a customer, and Jake and his friends were still where I left them. When they saw me, they perked up yet again, and I smiled.

"You boys enjoying yourselves?"

"Now that you're back, yes."

I smiled, glancing over my shoulder at Colin, whose teeth were tightly clenched, his eyes shooting daggers at me.

He'd once said I was playing a dangerous game. I was just realizing what he meant.

Chapter 6

I WAVED AT THE BOYS, who were the last to leave, and watched as Colin stormed behind them and closed the door. My pulse was erratic as I watched him, the anger evidently still sizzling off him.

"What did you achieve by playing in my face like that?" He asked as he made his way back.

"I wasn't playing—"

"I specifically told you not to entertain them," he spat.

"And why shouldn't I?" I asked. "I thought you said the key is to be engaging," I teased.

"You knew what you were doing," he said as he stopped in front of me. "You were trying to get a rise out of me."

I wanted to smile, but I didn't dare do it—not now. "Seems like it worked."

His jaw ticked. "Did you want to go home with one of them tonight?"

I frowned. "Of course not."

"Then it was pointless to lead them on when you know the only cock you'll be getting is mine."

I gasped, my heart hammering, my pussy flooding with juices as he spoke.

"I never doubted that," I said, and a ghost of a smile played in his mouth before he cupped my face in his hands and took me in a soul-shattering kiss. I moaned, grasping onto him as I kissed him back with as much urgency as he kissed me. I was already burning up from his kisses and could only imagine what it would be like to take things further.

I'd waited so long—wanted so long. I couldn't do a minute more. My fingers fumbled against his buckle as I searched for his cock. Only this time, there'd be a different destination.

I tore my mouth from him, gasping in impatience as I struggled to get him loose this time. Colin took over, prying my hands away while he got to release himself. He met my gaze, and my body burned as his scorching brown eyes met mine.

I unbuttoned my shorts and pulled them to my ankles, my panties next. As soon as I was about to peel off the straps of my blouse, Colin pulled me against him, and I landed on his hard body in an oomph. He caught my mouth yet again, kissing me hungrily, his tongue tracing my lips, my cheeks, my chin.

I moaned as I arched my neck and closed my eyes, allowing him to suckle on the column of my neck while his hard erection pressed against my stomach, hardening even more as he suckled on my skin.

"Yes," I breathed, reaching between us to hold his cock that was hot against my skin, throbbing against my tummy.

Colin spun me around, and I lost my grasp on it. It was now pressed against my ass. I craned my neck to the side and allowed him to continue his kisses there while his busy hands tightened around my breasts, squeezing them firmly and causing more juices to flow to my pussy.

I moaned, a small tremor passing through me when one hand trailed to my stomach, setting off the butterflies in it. My heart crashed against my chest when his hand slipped lower, passing over my prickly mound before he slid his middle finger down my slit.

I leaned over, shoving my ass further on him. Colin grunted, and my knees buckled when he slipped a finger inside me.

"Oh."

"As wet as that pretty little mouth," he said before he added another finger inside me, thrusting inside me and adjusting my pussy for his cock.

I whimpered as his skillful fingers stroked my flesh, inspiring more juices. He slipped it out and brought it up to my gaze, allowing me to see my juices smeared across his fingers, both fingers almost webbed together with cream.

Colin brought them to my mouth, and I sucked on them hard as if they were his cock. He grunted in approval before he slipped them inside my pussy again. I leaned against him, allowing him to finger fuck me while he used his other hand to caress my breast.

"Oh, I want you."

"Only me?" He asked, driving his finger deeper.

I gasped. "Only you..." I swallowed, my throat feeling parched. "It's always you," I said.

He licked across my ear, dragging his teeth along the lobe. "I want you to say that while I'm driving my cock past these thick pussy lips."

I nodded. "I'd do anything. I just want you inside me... please."

His hand slipped out and I reached for the counter to balance myself while he bent me over. He grabbed my ass cheeks and kneaded them into his hands, spreading them before he slapped them gently.

I was already weak in the knees, but when Colin began running his cock up and down my flesh from behind, I began to wonder if I'd have the strength to keep standing for long. His cock was firm against my sensitive pussy, spurring juices that were already emitting wet sounds.

I bit my lips as I braced myself when he pressed his cock to my entrance. He was so big, I could already tell even before he entered me.

I screamed when he filled me with one sinful thrust that had me gripping the counter for support. His lengthy groan mingled with mine. His grip tightening on my hips as he moved further and further inside me with each movement.

"Fuck, you feel good. So fucking good," he drawled before he began to withdraw. I felt everything, my snug walls clinging onto his intrusive length as he ripped me open.

I shifted my legs further apart, thinking I needed more room for my pussy to take him better. He filled me, and it felt like I could feel the way all in my stomach with each thrust.

"I don't think I'm gonna last, baby," he said. I didn't think I would last either, with how good he felt.

Colin plunged into me yet again before he bucked, his speed increasing before he filled me with his full length. I gasped, quickly steadying myself when he began filling me with his warm seed. His grunts were loud as he came, and my walls clung around his cock, collecting every drop while I basked in the sensation of being filled with cum.

"Oh fuck, you feel too good, Katie," he said as he pulled me up and turned me to face him. He kissed me searingly, his wet cock against my stomach while his cum dribbled from my slit and down my legs. I moaned against him, feeling dirty and loving every second of it. Colin had only come with a few thrusts, but I knew he had more up his sleeves. I could tell by the way he kissed me, the way he was still hard against me.

He broke the kiss. "Stay here."

Chapter 7

Colin

I'D TRIED, BUT THE second I entered Katie's pussy, I knew I didn't stand a chance. She was soft, and so fucking wet and tight that I just had to bust. Plus, with all the emotions from earlier, everything had just attacked me in full force. I couldn't resist her thick thighs, her juicy lips, her huge breasts. I didn't have it in me to be deep inside her for the first time and not bathe her with my cum in just a matter of seconds.

We kissed, and though I hadn't gone completely soft, I could feel my cock hardening against her soft skin. Every inch of her was soft. From her lips to her pussy, and I couldn't get enough.

She had those full lips you knew were soft before you even kissed them and boy, had I waited a long time to kiss them. She was the perfect woman, and in Mercury, she was like a diamond in the rough. My diamond.

I pulled away from her with my cock wet and hard from her juices. I got a towel from around back and laid it out against the pool table where we'd started off things earlier.

I glanced at Katie, who just stared from over the counter. Her face flushed, her hair slightly tousled, with a strap of her flimsy little blouse fallen to her shoulder. She looked edible, and as she walked from around the counter, the breath ceased in my throat.

My eyes traveled along her thick thighs—fucking thunderous—with a waistline that had no business being that small. Her nipples were visible against her blouse, one breast almost falling from her shirt.

I swallowed the lump in my throat as my gaze lingered on her pussy which was feathered with a light amount of hair. Her thick lips were still visible, and I swallowed, anticipating my cock tearing them apart.

I pulled her to me as soon as she was close enough and kissed her mouth yet again. She smelled like strawberries and vanilla, a beautiful scent that'd drive a man like me crazy.

I lifted her and placed her on the table, the towel beneath her. The other strap fell down her shoulders, and she slipped her hands from inside them, the small blouse now around her stomach. I drank in the sight of her tits, huge cups with big and beautifully pink areolas that surrounded a small hard nipple.

I licked across my lips. Katie opened her legs, and I lost it when I saw her pussy wet with my cum, some having trailed down her legs.

"Fuck," I whispered as I dragged my hands along her thick thighs before pulling her to me. My cock grazed against her pussy in doing so, and I didn't waste any time.

I plunged into her, enjoying her lips puckered as my cock reacquainted itself with her drenched walls.

Katie gasped, throwing her head back and spreading her thighs further apart.

"Look at me while I fuck you," I said, slipping my hand behind the small of her back so she was closer to me.

She met my gaze, her lips apart, her face flushed as I slammed into her. Her long dark hair bounced behind her as well as the tits on her chest as I fucked her.

Her pussy seemed impossibly sweeter, tainted with my cum to guide me even more freely inside her tightness. I looked between us as I rammed into her and noticed the cream that started to gather at the base of my cock. Katie's lips bobbed back and forth as I drilled her deep, forcing the remaining cum to spill from her.

"You like that, huh? You like me fucking you like my dirty little minx," I said, grabbing onto her neck.

"Yes, fuck me harder... please. I want more of your cum," she said between shaky breaths.

Her tight walls clung to me as I fucked her as if urging me to spill more cum for her, but it was Katie who was about to cum this time.

"Now it's time for you to flood my cock with your juices, baby," I said, slamming into her sweet pussy.

"Yes, Oh my God, yes! Colin!" She was whimpering, her cries broken, her body even more flushed as she neared her peak.

"Tell me you're mine, and I'll give you everything you want," I said between clenched teeth.

"Fuck, I am–I am yours for the rest of my life!" She cried, grabbing onto me. "I want your big cock inside me every day. You feel so good!"

Her pussy started to convulse around me, her words broken off by her piercing cry. She began to shake before she wriggled off my cock, her body trembling as I came.

I pulled my cock in my hand as I watched her, my teeth clenched as she writhed on the pool table.

I grunted, grabbing onto her leg while a blast of my cum fell between her legs. I pulled her up to me, my hands shaking as I directed the tip of my cock inside her, allowing her to get the remainder of my cum.

I threw my head back and groaned throatily while I emptied myself.

AFTER A FEW MINUTES, I picked Katie up from the pool table and carried her around the back room. She was smiling at me when I placed her on the bed and flicked on the lights.

"You're amazing," she said, her voice gone soft.

"You made me nut three times today. I think you're the amazing one."

She giggled. "I've wanted this for a long time, Colin. I've gotta say it was well worth the wait."

"We can agree on that," I said, combing back the hair from her pretty face.

"What do you mean?"

"I mean, I've wanted you before you stepped through that door the other day," I confessed.

Her eyes widened. "You did?"

"You were the first person to catch my attention when I moved to Mercury."

She beamed at me and eased up from the bed. "I was?"

I nodded.

"What, but you wouldn't even look my way."

"I knew you were young –"

"I was twenty-one. You said you didn't date *under twenty*."

"It's different in a place like this," I said.

"You're right, but I can't believe you found me attractive. I was so thin then and shy... innocent."

"I love the weight," I smiled, trailing my hands down her leg. You're attractive at any size, though."

"I wish you'd said something. At least I would have known."

I leaned it to kiss her. "Everything happens on its own time."

"You're right; I maybe would have changed my mind about college and stayed here to be your fuck doll."

I grinned. "I wouldn't have complained."

She got up and swung her legs over mine, her hands wrapped around my neck. She met my gaze, her green eyes glistening.

"Is it bad that I want you again?"

"Not when I want the same." I reached under her for my cock, and she lifted her ass before she lowered herself on it. She sighed heavily as she impaled herself on my rod, not stopping until she had the whole thing inside her.

I knew then I'd never get enough of this minx.

Chapter 8

COLIN WENT OUT THE following evening, too, and after last night, I missed him more than ever. He promised he'd be back before closing, which was soon, but I wouldn't be assured until he walked through that door.

The bar had a few people but wasn't as packed as the previous day. I had some time to catch my breath in between, and that was good enough for me. But each time I glanced over at the pool table surrounded by men, I couldn't help but remember last night and how well Colin had fucked me on it.

My cheeks warmed at the memory, desire shooting through me. Just the thought of Colin was able to get me wet, and I knew when he arrived, I'd be soaked.

I hummed to the music on the stereo as I wiped down the counter and collected the empty bottles they'd left behind.

I gasped when a man walked up to the counter with a smirk on his face that made my blood run cold. My heart hammered, and I swallowed the lump in my throat when I realized who he was.

He was the man who'd caught me and Colin the other day.

"Hey there, pretty lady," he said, folding his arms on his counter while his gaze trailed down my body. I felt disgusted and had only wanted Colin to look at me in that manner.

"Can I get you something, sir?"

His smile broadened as he leaned further in, looking from side to side as if to see if anyone was around.

He licked across his chapped lips. "How about the same thing you gave Colin the other day?"

I gasped, pulling back from him as my pulse raced.

"I'd prefer it all down your throat, though," he smiled.

My eyes pricked with tears. "Could you leave?"

He scoffed. "Come on now, I promise to keep this a secret as well." He dragged his finger across his closed lips, imitating a sealed mouth.

"No thanks. Now, I don't know who the hell you think I am, but it's not what you're thinking."

"Oh, please. Everyone here knows you obviously didn't come back from the city as innocent as you left. I know that for a fact," he chuckled. "Those pretty lips probably sucked every city college boy's dick. I'd probably get lost in the count."

My lips quivered with anger. "Get the fuck out of here before I call the Sheriff. You wouldn't get a second with me if you were the last man on earth."

His mouth twisted in surprise, but he remained silent, then walked away. I had a feeling he would stir up trouble down the line.

COLIN'S MOTORCYCLE pulled up just as I was about to close the front door. I smiled as soon as I saw him and leaned against the doorpost, watching him as he took his helmet off and approached me.

"You're late," I said, still smiling.

"Seems to me I'm just in time," he said, wrapping his hands around me and kissing me.

Everything I felt for Colin immediately came to the surface, desire filling me in just an instant.

"Come, I'm taking you to my place," he said.

"You are?"

He nodded, and I giggled as I rushed to the counter to collect my things. Since my car wasn't fixed as yet, Colin had been my source of transportation at nights. I hopped on the back of his motorcycle and clung onto him as he started the motorcycle and drove off.

There wasn't any hesitance this time or nervousness on my part. Colin and I'd been together, and I felt no shame in wrapping my hands around him and claiming him like he was my man. I breathed in his scent, the cool wind in my hair, and Colin providing me with some level of warmth.

He didn't ride far, and when he stopped, it occurred to me that this was the first time I'd see his home. It was small with a porch with a swinging chair beneath it.

Years ago, this was an old woman's house, but she passed, and the place had been abandoned for a while. I was just realizing Colin was the one who bought it.

We entered his house, and he kicked off his boots while my eyes traveled around his manly den. The interior was mostly brown undertones, giving it a kind of rustic farmhouse look. The air wreaked of his scent, which was that woodsy, musky scent that would make any girl swoon.

Everything was in order, which was no surprise since he always showed how clean he was at the bar.

He turned to me, catching me staring.

"I missed you," he said as he pulled me to him, his brown eyes meeting mine.

"Show me," I said, smiling up at him. "I have a few minutes before I have to leave."

"Stay," he said.

"I can't. My mom would have a fit."

He chuckled and lowered his lips to mine. My eyes closed as soon as his soft lips touched mine. I wrapped my hands around his neck, caressing his tongue with mine and feeling my desire thrum between my legs.

Colin's hand trailed down my back and around my ass, squeezing it and causing me to press further into him, where I felt his growing erection. I moaned against his lips, feeling a similar sensation all over my body as his soft lips molded mine.

He picked me up while I kissed him and carried us somewhere. I glimpsed the bed in the background and realized it was his bedroom. He placed me on my feet and I immediately got to discarding my clothes. Colin did the same and was faster than me. As I was peeling off my panties, he was already seated on the bed, stroking his cock in hand.

I was struck breathless when I saw him there, every inch of his muscle, tattoos all over his body while his naked cock readied itself for me.

He looked at me like a predator, and I was his prey. His eyes were darker as they trailed down my body as if stamping every inch of me to memory.

I moved towards him and swung my legs over, raising my ass before slowly impaling myself on his thick cock. I grunted as inch after inch escaped inside me. Colin's moan was long, his hands on my hips as he sunk me further down on his length. I gasped, grabbing onto his shoulder as he filled me up.

Colin grabbed my head and gave me a searing kiss to stifle my moans as I swallowed up his length. My walls clung to him as we kissed, my walls massaging his thick girth as it throbbed inside me.

Colin licked across my mouth and kissed my chin before he went to suckle on my neck. I threw my head back and whimpered as pleasure consumed me entirely. His hands were hot against my body, leaving a trail of heat everywhere he touched.

I began to slowly rock my hips against him, wanting to feel more of him as the pleasure increased inside me. Colin continued to kiss along my neck, holding me in place before he slid his mouth to my breast and caught a nipple in his mouth. I whimpered, closing my eyes, my walls involuntarily clenching around him his sweet cock. He grunted simultaneously, shifting his body, which made his length lurch further inside me.

"That's right, baby," he said as my tits before he licked across my flesh yet again.

I went faster, riding him, my pussy filled to its fullest with his cock. Colin muttered something indecipherable as he began pulling my hips, aiding my movements while I rocked back and forth on his cock.

"Come for me, baby," he said, and I gasped, my grip tightening on him while the pleasure crescendoed inside me. I grunted while my pussy began to convulse around Colin. As the pleasure heightened inside me, so did my cries as I clung around his cock.

A tremor passed through me, and my body stiffened, my cunt gripping Colin's cock tightly. My body jerked, and I cried when a bolt of pleasure crashed into me. I was so lost in my own pleasure that it took me a couple of seconds to realize Colin was grunting loudly, too. He twitched inside me, and as I came, he joined me, filling me with his thick cum. He buried his face in my busty bosom, holding me tight as his warm essence filled my insides. I clung to him, my body shaking as we rose to the peak of our orgasm.

A minute later when, I climbed off him and flopped down in the bed, slightly exhausted from my orgasm. Colin laid beside me on the bed, placing a kiss on my cheeks.

"I won't ever be able to get enough of you," he said as he wrapped his hand around me and pulled me closer to him.

"I wouldn't want you to."

He smiled, and we lay there in momentary silence while I tried to get my thoughts together.

"Why did you come to Mercury?" I asked him, wanting to know more about him besides his body.

Colin pulled in a breath. "I was born and raised in Chicago, but after a while, the city gets lonely. I didn't want to be there at the time."

I turned to him. "I didn't know you came from the City."

He nodded. "I did."

"Do you love it here?"

"I liked it here; now I love it," he said as he glanced at me, a smirk on his face.

I smiled. "I'd forgotten how exhausting Mercury was until I got back. I loved being in LA, but a part of me always wanted to be back home, but now I don't know."

"What's on your mind, Katie?" He asked me, and my pulse picked up pace. I turned to him and saw the concern on his face.

"The guy that caught us at the bar the other day, he came there tonight and..." I cleared my throat. "He said some things to me—nasty things, and there's just this feeling in my gut that he's gonna cause trouble, y'know. And I don't think I could live it down if he tells anybody. People here are so close-minded."

Colin frowned. "That son of a bitch!" He spat as he bounded upright. "I fucking told him not to say anything."

I reached for his shoulder. "I don't know that he will," I said as I sat up beside him. "And quite frankly, I wouldn't even care if he told the whole world. It's just my family I'm worried about."

He looked at me. "You wouldn't care?"

"I've wanted you for a long time, Colin. I would fuck you in front of an audience if it meant them knowing I'm yours."

A glint flashed across his eyes. "You would?"

"I would," I whispered. "I'm yours, aren't I?"

"More than you know," he said as he tilted my chin towards his and kissed me softly on the lips. I already felt the desire rushing through me despite coming just minutes ago. But Colin could always make me aroused by a look or even a simple touch.

My stomach stirred with emotions as his hands trailed down my arm before he slipped below and grabbed my hips, pulling me closer to him.

We kissed, his hands between my legs, gently stroking my flesh as he moved closer and closer to my pussy. As he touched my sensitive flesh, I quivered, a wave of arousal passing through me. Colin moaned against my mouth, and I deepened the kiss as he slid two fingers inside me, parting my flesh and stroking my walls.

I whimpered, grabbing onto his flexing arms as he caressed my flesh. The wetness was still evident and audible as his fingers moved inside me.

I wanted him inside me, I wanted him to fill me and stretch me, and I wanted it now.

I rested my back against the pillows while Colin came between my legs. He kissed my lips and my cheek, and he kissed my neck. I felt his cock grazing against my legs in the process, brushing against my pussy. I pried my legs further apart, wanting to give him full access to fuck me.

I gasped when his cock slid against my flesh again, and after a while, when my gasps became constant, I realized he was doing so purposefully. I smiled and reached around to grab his firm ass, pressing him further against me. He slid against my wet, slippery slit, his hips rocking as he teased me with his firm length.

"Now," I said, growing impatient, between my legs flooded with my juices.

Colin didn't comply right away. He continued to rub his hard girth up and down my slit until I was sure I was about to cum. As my moans increased, my nails digging into his skin, he slid inside me, stretching me to the max as his cock massaged my walls.

I grunted, my breathing labored as Colin slid further inside me, ramming his cock deeper each time until he was at the hilt.

"Oh fuck me, please," I begged, clawing at his face to taste his kisses.

He only kissed me briefly on the lips before he propped himself up on his knees and held my legs apart. I stared at him as he towered over me, pure muscle as he moved inside me.

I tossed my head from side to side as Colin slammed into me, each thrust punctuated with a grunt. I already began to clench and unclench around him, and I knew I wasn't far from my orgasm.

Colin paused, and I gasped, staring up at him questionably.

As wet as I was, he allowed a dollop of spit to fall from his mouth and on his cock. I gasped as he then slammed into me, my pussy making squelching sounds as his length barreled through me.

"I love it when you're fucking soaking wet," he said between clenched teeth, his grip tightening on my thighs as he fucked me hard and deep.

My tits jiggled in my chest, bouncing so high they almost touched my chin. The mattress squeaked, and the headboard slammed against the wall while my cries filled the entire room. Colin didn't stop, and my pussy burned from his thrusts, but there was no greater feeling.

His chest glistened with sweat, his neck red, and his muscles bulking as he plunged into me.

"Colin!" I cried as he fucked me hard and rough.

"You like that baby! You like being fucked like a dirty little minx?"

"Y-yes!" I gasped, reaching for him.

He only reached out to grab one of my breasts, his hands holding it in place while the other one bounced swiftly in my chest. He didn't let up, and I felt like I was about to lose my mind as he moved inside me.

My orgasm crashed into me unexpectedly, and my legs threatened to close up around him, but Colin quickly tore his hand away from my breast and held the other leg apart. He slowed his pace slightly, but while my orgasm crashed into me over and over, he still continued to fuck me, and I was near to losing my mind. Just as one orgasm passed through me, another came, and I feared I'd pass out from a third one.

Colin fucked me swiftly, grunting loudly before he quickly pulled out. A spurt of cum immediately surged from his cock as soon as he pulled out, landing over my breasts. I was still breathing heavily as he came, filling my stomach with his warm seed. I reached down and used my finger to smear it all over my mound and belly button until Colin was done emptying himself.

He fell beside me, exhausted, and I smiled, unable to move. My heart rejoiced at the happiness I felt, and I didn't want it to be over. It was too good. I didn't even know when I fell asleep, but I knew it was shortly after we'd come.

Chapter 9

I YAWNED, A SMILE ON my face as my eyes fluttered open. I knew where I was because even in my dreams, Colin held the focus. I knew I was waking up beside him, but to really be in the position made me even happier.

I turned to face him and realized he was up, watching me, a small smile on his face.

I blushed. "Good morning."

"Good morning, sleeping beauty," he said.

I giggled. "Please. I must look like I'd been run over by a car." He chuckled. "Far from it."

I reached up to kiss him, and he kissed me back more passionately than I had anticipated.

"What time is it?" I asked, yawning yet again.

"Ten."

My eyes widened, and I quickly bounded upright. "Shit, I overslept. I should head home," I said, searching for my clothes.

"I'm sure your parents already knew you didn't come home last night," he argued.

"I know, but this is worse." I paused to look down on myself. I felt sticking and dirty, and there was dried cum all over my body. "Shit, I have to take a shower."

"You're more than welcome to use mine if you allow me to join," he smirked.

I smiled. "I'd love nothing more, but you'll only make me later than I already am."

"Go," he simply said, and I quickly collected my things and rushed towards the door.

I didn't know where Colin's bathroom was, but I found it as soon as I left the room. I made the shower run while I peed and then later stepped inside. His soaps all smelled like him—noticeably masculine. I smiled as I lathered myself in his scent, knowing I'd still smell like him even after I left here.

Once done, I pulled on my clothes and piled my hair in a bun on the top of my head.

When I entered Colin's bedroom, he had pulled on boxers, but he still looked so yummy I wished I didn't have to leave.

"I'll see you later?"

"You will. I'll be at the bar the whole time tonight." I moved towards him and kissed him quickly on the lips. I was about to pull away when he grabbed my hand and pulled me to him, crashing his mouth to mine. I felt the effects all the way in my knees, which suddenly felt weak from his passionate kiss. My nipples tightened, and my body became heated just from a single kiss.

"That feels like a promise."

He chuckled. "Definitely is."

I smiled and said my goodbyes before I left his house. It was bright outside and I was just happy Colin lived further away from most of the houses. No one was out in this area; the sun was out, and it was a perfect time to walk home. The last thing I wanted was for my parents to see Colin dropping me off the morning after.

I WAS IN A GOOD MOOD as I walked towards my house, but knew it would be short-lived because my parents would drill me about why I was coming home at almost midday.

I paused once I stepped into my walkway, my heart pumping when I saw my suitcase on the porch. I ran towards the house and pushed the door open, wanting to confront my mom about what was happening. They couldn't be serious.

I stopped in my tracks when I entered the living room, and she stood there as if waiting for me. Her face was marred with disgust, her mouth downturned in a scowl while her eyes trailed my frame with utter scorn.

I frowned. "What's my suitcase doing outside?" I asked.

"You even have the nerve to ask me that?" She asked as her frown deepened.

"Mom, I'm twenty-five years old. You can't think that I'll be cooped up in the house all day. Plus, this is the first time I've ever done something like this?"

She scoffed. "You think this is because you're just coming home?"

I stared at her, realizing there was a bigger issue at hand.

"I went to the store this morning only to find people gossiping behind my back and shaking their heads in pity. I thought it was something I'd done, only to find out that you were caught in a bar like a damn prostitute with a man's seed spilling all over your face!"

I gasped, taking a step back as the world suddenly began to spin around me. I grabbed onto the sofa for balance while my blurry gaze searched the floor.

"You can't even deny it!" Her voice broke. "I want you out of this house right now. I won't suffer from your disgrace. You can't even begin to imagine what that'll do to your father."

I looked up at her. "I'm sorry."

She scoffed. "And you think that's about to make things better? I don't even know who you are anymore!" She exclaimed.

"Mom, I'm the same person," I defended, tears spilling down my face.

"The daughter that left here years ago isn't the one that's here now. I certainly didn't raise a prostitute!"

I gasped, taken aback by her words, but also knew she wouldn't see reason—not now or maybe never. Like most of the others in Mercury, people like my mom were quite stuck in their ways and wouldn't see the light of day no matter what.

With a heavy heart, I left and went to the porch where she'd managed to cram my entire life in a suitcase. My lips quivered as I stared down at it, wondering where I'd go now. I didn't even have my car back, and I definitely couldn't struggle with my suitcase back in town.

As much as I didn't want to at the moment, Colin was the only person I thought of calling.

I sniffled when he answered. "Hey baby, you okay?"

I wanted to cry even more at his softness. "My mom kicked me out," I croaked. "She found out about what happened at the bar, and apparently, the whole town knows now," I cried.

He was silent on the other end for a second, and I wondered if he'd hung up. "I'll be there in ten minutes." The softness had gone from his voice, and I wondered why. He sounded angry. Just as I was about to ask what was wrong, he hung up.

I cried as I sat on the chair on the porch, picking at my fingers while I waited for Colin to arrive.

The door opened, and my heart lurched, thinking it was my mom, but it was Emma. I quickly wiped the tears from my face but knew she already saw me crying.

"I didn't know you were here?" I said, clearing my throat.

She came to take a seat beside me, looking to the road. "You like this guy?"

I nodded, lips quivering. "I do," I croaked.

She looked towards me and smiled. "I saw him once at the store. He's handsome."

I couldn't help my smile. "He is."

"This town doesn't have a lot of handsome guys, but he is. You're lucky."

I bumped her shoulder. "What do you know?" I grinned.

"You should run away with him. This shitty town has nothing to offer but tumbleweeds and regrets."

"Do you hate it here?"

Emma scoffed. "I always wondered why you came back. You had the perfect opportunity to spread your wings, and you came back to this straight jacket of a town."

I pulled in a breath. "I didn't realize how draining it was until I got back. Plus, my main reason was to see Colin again."

She smiled and looked at me. "You've changed in a good way, Katie. Don't let this place make you feel like you're some alien or somethin' for being different. Everyone's so boring. They don't worry about a single thing as long as their guts are fed. You're smart and brave, and you should be somewhere that appreciates that."

I found myself crying all over again. I nodded as I glanced at Emma. I pulled her in for a hug, crying against her shoulders.

"Thank you."

COLIN CAME, AND AS horrible as I felt earlier, I now felt hopeful. Emma was never one to talk much—in fact, we were never really close growing up, but today, she was exactly what I needed.

I smiled as Colin parked along the side of the road. He was driving my car, which seemed to be fixed. That made me happier. He jumped out and moved towards me, looking straight at me.

Something shot through my heart, and it felt almost overwhelming. I realized then that it was more than just lust. I was in love with this man and that I had probably been for a long time. My heart soared in my chest as he approached me and pulled me into his arms. I felt the need to cry again, but the happiness that bubbled in my chest outweighed the sadness I'd felt earlier. He kissed me softly before he reached down to grab my suitcase. He paused when he saw Emma, who sat there beaming.

"Hi," he said.

Emma grinned. "You better make her happy."

He chuckled. "I damn sure will."

She giggled.

I hugged Emma again before I walked towards the car. Colin placed my suitcase in the back before he joined me in the front. My gaze went to his bruised knuckles as he held the steering wheel, and I gasped.

"What happened?"

"It's nothing," he said, flexing his fingers.

"Colin?"

He looked at me. "I showed that asshole not to mess with what's mine."

With that, he started the ignition and drove off. "Where do you wanna go?" he asked while I eased back in the seats.

"Anywhere but here at the moment."

"In that case, I think I'll have to pack a suitcase too, then."

I whipped my gaze towards him. "Wh– you're serious?"

He glanced at me, smiling. "As a judge. Pick a place, and we'll go there for as long as you want."

My eyes were wide. "What about the bar?"

He shrugged. "That's the last thing on my mind right now, baby."

I grinned. "What's the first thing?"

He reached over to hold my hand. "You... always."

I'd been spontaneous in my life, but this broke the record completely. It all became more real when Colin packed his suitcase and threw it in the back with mine.

My heart skipped a beat, excitement filling me when we drove past the sign an hour later that read;

You're now leaving Mercury.

Epilogue

2 years later

EVER SINCE COLIN AND I packed our things and decided to leave Mercury, I hadn't gone back. Colin went back to sort out things with the bar and put his place up for rent, but I hadn't been back since.

I'd chosen Chicago, and here we were a year later. I was happy and in love—what more could a girl like me want? Colin was looking into opening a club while I worked HR for a prominent business in the city. We were definitely getting by.

I smiled as I looked from the floor-to-ceiling windows that overlooked the busy city. I thought about the vast difference to Mercury, which was small and quiet. I was meant to be in a place like this with the love of my life. After all, this was the place where I found myself and discovered the true me, and I'd always be grateful for that.

I closed my eyes, warmth spreading across my stomach when Colin wrapped his huge hands around me. I smiled, leaning back against him, clinging onto that feeling of safety that he brought me:

"We should start getting ready. We don't want to miss your sister's graduation," he said, kissing me on the ear.

"Mmm, you're right," I said, turning to him and reaching up to kiss him.

"Are you prepared for it?" He asked me.

"I am," I smiled. "I've had a lot of time to prepare myself."

He raised my hand and kissed the diamond on my finger. "And what about this?"

I glanced at the glistening diamond ring. "I'm sure Emma told them. They just don't give a damn, babe." I kissed him on the lips before I moved to get my dress from the closet.

I then went to the bathroom to shower, pondering what Colin had asked. My parents had proven time and time again that they were done with me. The fact that I left Mercury made that worse, and though I'd tried to reach out, it was just always them telling me about how disappointed they were in me and how I'd scandalized the family name in their small town.

After a while, I'd grown tired of them not reciprocating the energy I offered and had stopped completely. Emma was the only one I spoke to, and quite frankly, I was quite contented with that as the time passed. I just wanted to be surrounded by people who were cheering for me, and they weren't.

OUR DRIVE BACK TO MERCURY felt long, and the closer we came to entering the town, the more exhausted I started to feel.

I looked to Colin, who I found comfort in seeing, and smiled, trying to calm my nerves. He reached over to give my hand a reassuring squeeze, and I lifted it to my lips, kissing him there.

"I love you, you know that?" He asked.

"I know, baby. You make it a habit to tell me every day," I said.

He chuckled.

"I love you too."

People already started to look as we drove up to Emma's school. There weren't many of them outside, but they realized the car was unfamiliar, so they just had to see who it was.

I glanced at my watch as Colin parked and realized we were some minutes late. I quickly got out, seeing the shock on their faces as we stepped out of the vehicle.

Colin adjusted his tie and held my hand. We went inside the school's auditorium, already hearing someone talking on the speaker even before we entered.

When Colin pushed the huge double doors open, they squeaked, alerting everyone inside the huge room. My heart fluttered as heads turned to look, chatter quickly escalating.

I blew out a small sigh, my hand tightening around Colin's as we sought out the chairs Emma said she'd reserved.

A hand lifted in the air, and I was quite surprised to find it was my dad's. They sat all the way up to the front, behind the graduates. The walk seemed endless, my heels clicking loudly inside the mostly silent room.

I sighed heavily once I arrived and sat down beside my dad. Mom was on the other side beside him, her gaze narrowed ahead.

"Hey, Dad," I said, smiling.

He looked about to cry, and I didn't know if I was seeing things, but he looked proud.

"It's good to see you, Honey," he said, reaching for my hand.

"It's great to see you too." I looked ahead and spotted Emma looking back at us. She had a huge smile on her face, and I smiled back, sending her a quick wave.

I could sense the gaze fixed on me, even as I sat there with my back turned to the most. If it hadn't been for Colin sitting beside me, I maybe would have walked out, but I quickly reminded myself I was here for Emma.

Once everything ended, people started to get up to greet the graduates. I spotted Emma boring her way through the crowd, and I grinned as I moved to greet her. I hugged her tightly, happy to see her after many months.

"I'm glad you came," she said.

"I wouldn't miss it for the world," I said. "Congrats, by the way. You did a fabulous as valedictorian."

She blushed. "What can I say? I love following in my sister's footsteps."

"Oh, don't let Mom hear that," I whispered, and we both burst out laughing.

"Congratulations, honey," Dad said as he came towards us. People still passed, staring at us blatantly, not even hiding the fact that they were gossiping while doing so.

He turned to me. "It's really nice to have you back, Katie. Emma told us about the great things you're doing in the city."

I cleared my throat. "Yeah, life's great."

He turned to my mom who still chose to stay at a distance. "Your mom wants to say something," he said, pulling her towards him.

I straightened, preparing myself for whatever was to come.

She couldn't meet my eyes, and she looked flustered.

"I'm sorry," she said, but with the noise in the auditorium, I almost missed it.

She finally looked up at me, her eyes glossy with tears. "Please forgive me; I'm sorry I was such a horrible mother to you."

My heart swelled in my chest, seeing her so vulnerable, which wasn't a quality she possessed.

"I missed you so much!" She said, pulling me into her for a hug. I hugged her back because, as horrible as things had been between us in the past, she was still my mom, and I could feel the remorse even as we hugged. I knew she was genuinely sorry, and that was all that mattered.

I was shocked when she pulled away from me and went to Colin, who she hugged with the same enthusiasm.

"Thank you for taking care of our baby girl," she said, voice shaky.

I laughed, brushing the tears from my face as we took turns hugging each other. I rotated back to Colin, who held me tight as if he didn't want to let me go.

I realized it didn't matter where I went. He'd always be home.

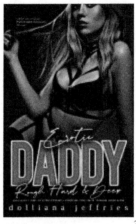

---

1. https://www.amazon.com/dp/B0C4X5X1ZJ

2. https://www.amazon.com/dp/B0C4X5X1ZJ

3. https://www.amazon.com/dp/B0C4X5X1ZJ

4. https://www.amazon.com/dp/B0C4X5X1ZJ

5. https://www.amazon.com/s?k=izzie+vee

Each book is sold for $2.99 or $0.99 individually. A no-brainer deal. Grab yours.

10 NOVELLAS COLLECTION[6]

[7]

CLICK HERE TO DOWNLOAD[8]

AN EXTRA STEAMY 10 BOOKS BOX SET

Get the first 10 stories in this series in one quick download.

These stories are insta-love, fast paced standalones that can be read in any order. All are extremely steamy and have a HEA ending.

Some of the themes are age-gap/older man younger woman romance, enemies to lovers, bully romance, grumpy boss, huge mountain man and more ...

List of stories inside:

1. Daddy's Taboo Family-Friend.
2. Possessive Alpha-Daddy

---

6. https://www.amazon.com/dp/B0BVC73GP3

7. https://www.amazon.com/dp/B0BVC73GP3

8. https://www.amazon.com/dp/B0BVC73GP3

Get your copy HERE[9]

Let's connect.

Get this book for **FREE**[10] when you sign up for our newsletter.

DARK & FILTHY!

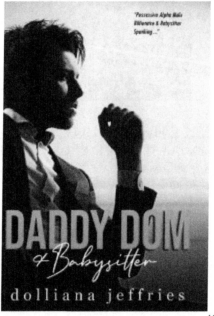

11

---

9. https://www.amazon.com/dp/B0BVC73GP3

10. https://www.subscribepage.com/b5r0y8

CLICK HERE TO GET FOR FREE[12]
WHEN BREAKING RULES LEADS TO BE BROKEN IN.

Older, filthy rich with a ***dark mystery*** to him.

No wonder he had rules. Well, just one rule.

Only one simple rule while working at his mansion.

The perks for working with him are wonderful, plus the pay is great.

A much-needed perk for a ***young college*** student like me.

Then why am I so drawn to break my boss's only rule?

He's stern, strict and seems the type to ***punish and discipline***, but still ...

There's something pulling me. To break his rule.

What will happen if he ever finds out what a naughty girl I've been?

GET YOUR FREE COPY HERE[13]